A Finnish Farmboy's Christmas

Garrett

Hyvää Joulua!

Sherri Majamaki

A Finnish Farmboy's Christmas

A Christmas Memory

Sherri Majamaki

Illustrated by Andrea Montano

A Finnish Farmboy's Christmas © 2017 Sherri Majamaki. All rights reserved. No part of this book may be used or reproduced in any manner whatsoever without written permission of the author, except in the case of brief quotations embodied in critical articles and reviews.

ISBN: 9-781946-195128

Library of Congress Control Number:
2017944532

Printed in the United States of America

First Printing 2017

21 20 19 18 17   5 4 3 2 1

Cover Design & Interior Book Design: FuzionPress

Printing by FuzionPress

1250 E 115th Street, Burnsville, MN, 55337 USA

FUZION PRESS

To order books email sherrimoore92@msn.com

This book is dedicated to Kayla, Thor, and Giselle.

I love you all, my darlings.

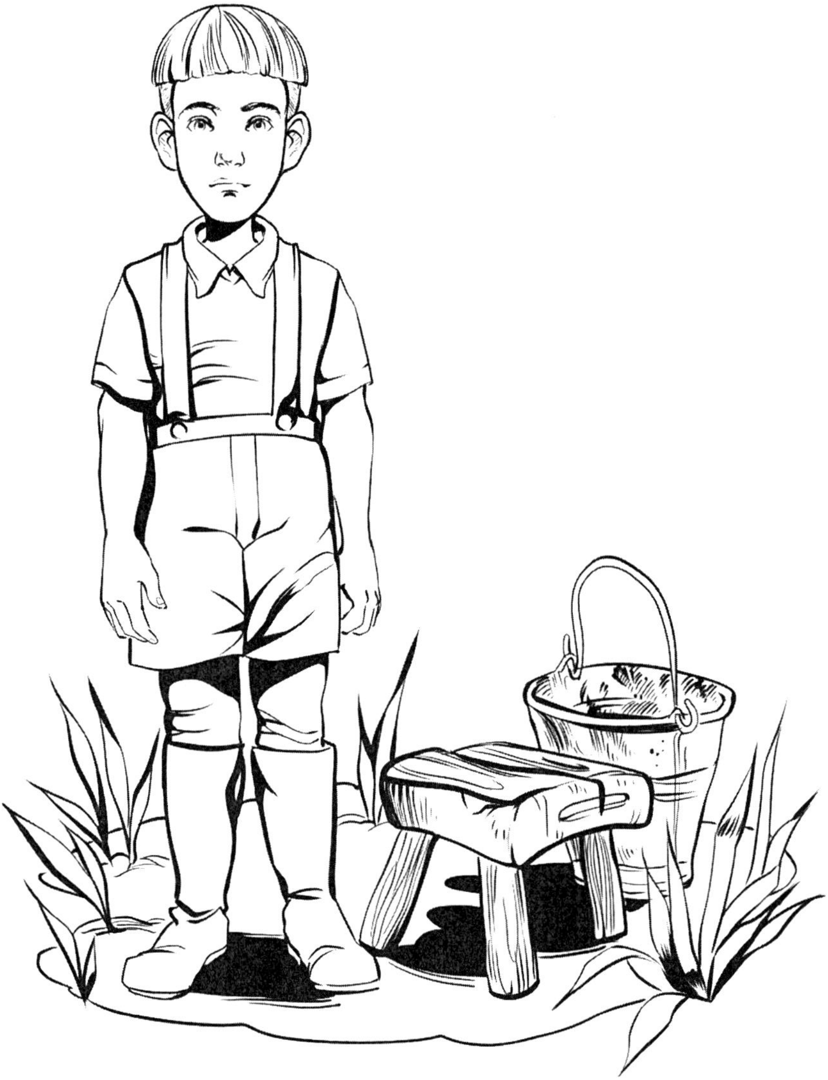

Chapter One

Markku and his family lived on a farm in Niinisalo, Finland. He liked being in the barn alone. The sun was setting, and light was shining in from the crack at the bottom of the door. He was done with his chores for today. He had fed the cows their hay, pigs their slop, and laid fresh straw in the stalls, too.

He put on his jacket, cap, and mittens, closed the barn door and pulled down the wooden latch. He thought about his mother and how she had said it was too much work for him. His older brothers earned money for the family, so Markku wanted to help too.

He walked past the outhouse and sauna to the kitchen door. Someone had already shoveled today's snowfall. He was relieved as he was too tired to shovel.

He stepped into the mudroom, removed his boots, then hung his jacket and cap on his hook. There were thirteen hooks on the wall, one for each of them. Markku had ten brothers and sisters, five older, and five younger. In his town, there were many big families and they all owned farms. His father once said, "Finland could be called the land of small farms and big families."

In the big room, the long table was set for dinner. His mother and sisters were busy getting the food ready to serve. Tonight was his favorite Saturday night dinner; mashed potatoes with meat sauce and carrots. His mother was a good cook. His work had made him hungry, and he had been looking forward to his favorite dinner all day. Mother turned and looked at him, "Markku, sit here by the stove. You need to warm up."

"Mother, I want to sit next to my brothers."

Markku knew they would try to push him off the end of the bench, but he was sure he could stop them tonight. He was getting stronger every day. He could not wait for the day when he could hold his seat on the end of the bench.

"No, do as I say."

He sat down next to his younger sister, Tetta. He knew he had to mind his mother.

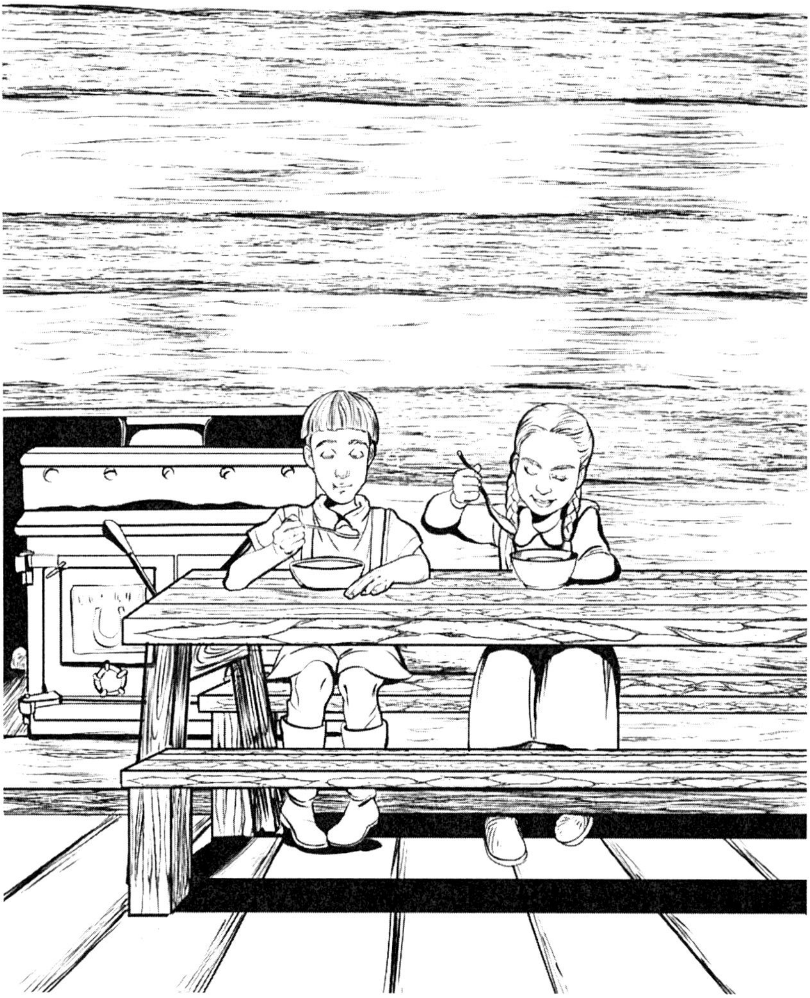

Chapter Two

The loud noise outside meant his father and brothers had returned from the forest. Through the window, he saw them brush the snow from their boots with a broom before entering the mud room. They all removed their jackets, hats, and gloves, then hung them on their hooks. All the hooks were filled.

Mother turned from the stove and greeted them. She looked at their father, "How was the work today? Did you cut down many trees?"

"Yes, we did. Today was a good day. We made good wages."

His mother sat at the end of the table and started dishing the food onto the plates, then passing them down, the first one going to their father. Next, she served the big boys who had been working all day, then Markku and the younger kids. They were all hungry but waited patiently for their plate of food.

Markku wanted to be tough like his father and brothers. They were farmers in the summer and lumberjacks in the winter. He wanted to be in the forest with them, cutting down trees. It was a quiet, magical place, where he could imagine anything. He thought of Vikings, running through the forest with their swords raised, knights on large horses, or trees coming alive and waving their branches.

His thoughts tonight were about how sick he had been this winter. He had three colds and sore throats. Then last month he got a very bad flu. His mother called the neighbor lady over to look at him. She had been a nurse during the war. She said it was not pneumonia, but he should stay home from school, drink warm black currant tea, and rest. So, he spent the days with his mother, little brother Hannu, sister Tetta and the two baby girls, Sirpa and Pirkko. He liked staying home when his older brothers and sisters were gone. While his brother and the girls napped, his mother whispered to him and wiped a cool cloth over his feverish face.

"It has been decided you will not work with your brothers. You are not strong enough to cut trees. The work is cold and wet. You will go to high school. You are good at math and reading, and I know you will do well."

His mother worried about him. He could see the sadness in her eyes when she took care of him. He liked school but wanted to earn money working with his brothers in the forest.

There were not enough beds for all the kids. The babies slept in the cardboard beds they received at the hospital. The government gave each new baby a bed, packed with diapers and clothes. The older kids slept on the floor on mats, like big pillow cases stuffed with straw. They all had warm blankets to pile on. His older brothers and sisters slept up in the attic, but he did not. He slept on the floor of the main room by the stove, with his younger brother and sisters. He wanted to sleep in the attic, but his mother said, "In June when it is warm, you can join them."

He could not wait for summer and warmer weather. This spring, he would be old enough to help with the planting. But for now, he would have to work at getting back to school.

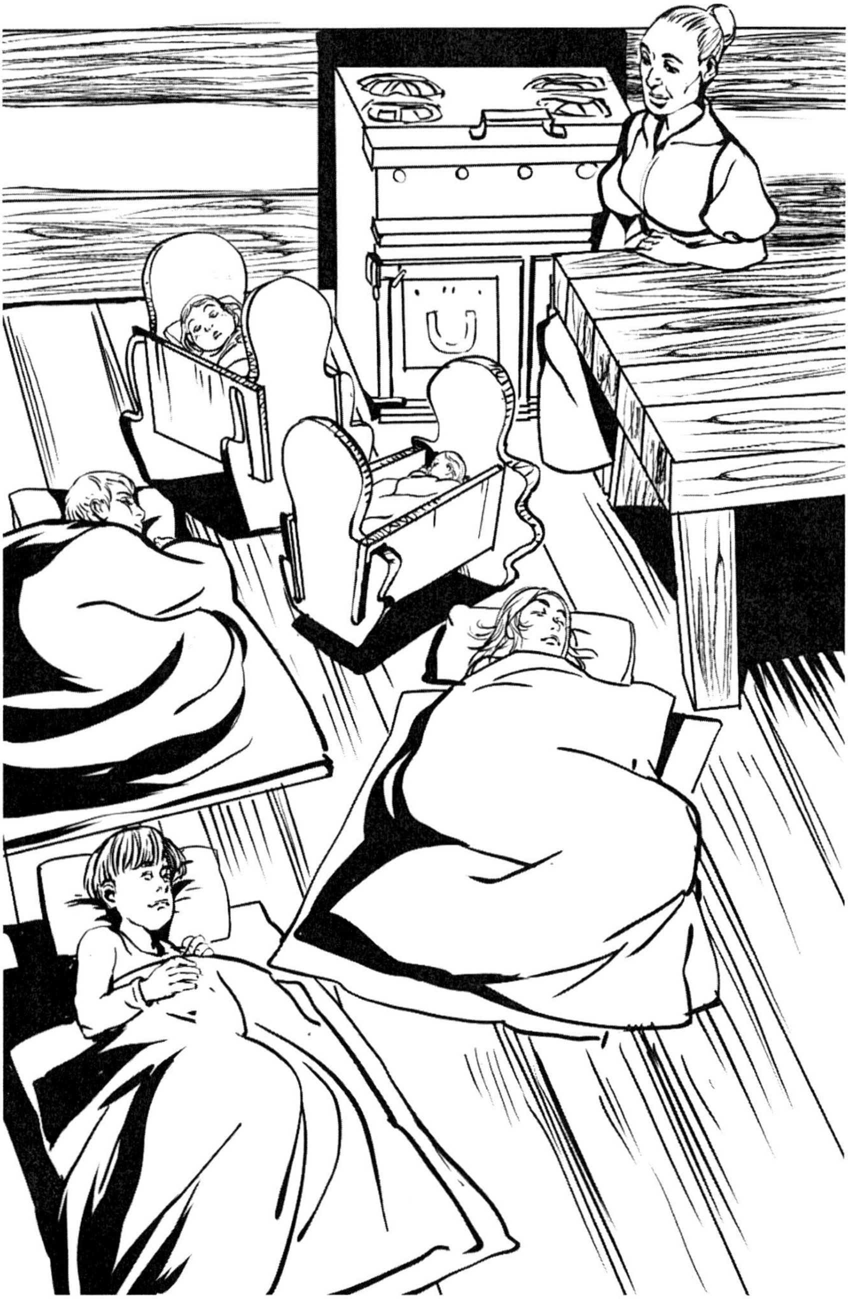

16

Chapter Three

The day finally came when Markku skied to school with his older sister. There were no school busses. All school children skied to school. It was fast and fun. He felt good gliding along in the snow.

His best friend Kauko and his other classmates welcomed him back. The teacher smiled as he took his seat. He smiled too and punched his friend in the arm as he sat down. They both laughed a little.

At recess, he asked Kauko and his sister, Seija if they knew of a job for him. "Do you need help on your farm? I want to buy my mother a Christmas gift."

"I do not know if there is anything we need help with. I will ask my mother."

Seija said, "Kauko, you lazy boy, we do not need Markku's help, but we need you to work harder."

Seija was always crabby to her brother. She often complained of how much work she did. Kauko mostly ignored her. She asked, "What kind of work can you do Markku?" She smiled when she talked to him.

"I can feed the animals and rake out the stalls. Sometimes I shovel. I bring in wood and buckets of water for the stove, too." He did not tell her his mother thought he was too weak to endure the cold and wet of working in the forest.

Kauko thought while he carefully rolled a snowball in his hands. "I think Seija likes you."

Markku turned and threw the snowball at Seija, hitting her in the back as she stomped into school. "I do not think I want a crabby girlfriend. I am tired enough of my sisters."

They both laughed as she yelled.

The next day after school, Kauko had to stay and be tutored. Markku skied part way home with Seija. "My mother asked me to tell you she could use your help with the animals on Wednesdays. She goes to town to visit Grandma in the hospital. She would like to stay with our aunt overnight and come home the next morning. Mother has no money, but she can make something nice for your mother. She is good at sewing and knitting. She said you could come home with me tomorrow after school."

"Thank you; I will do that."

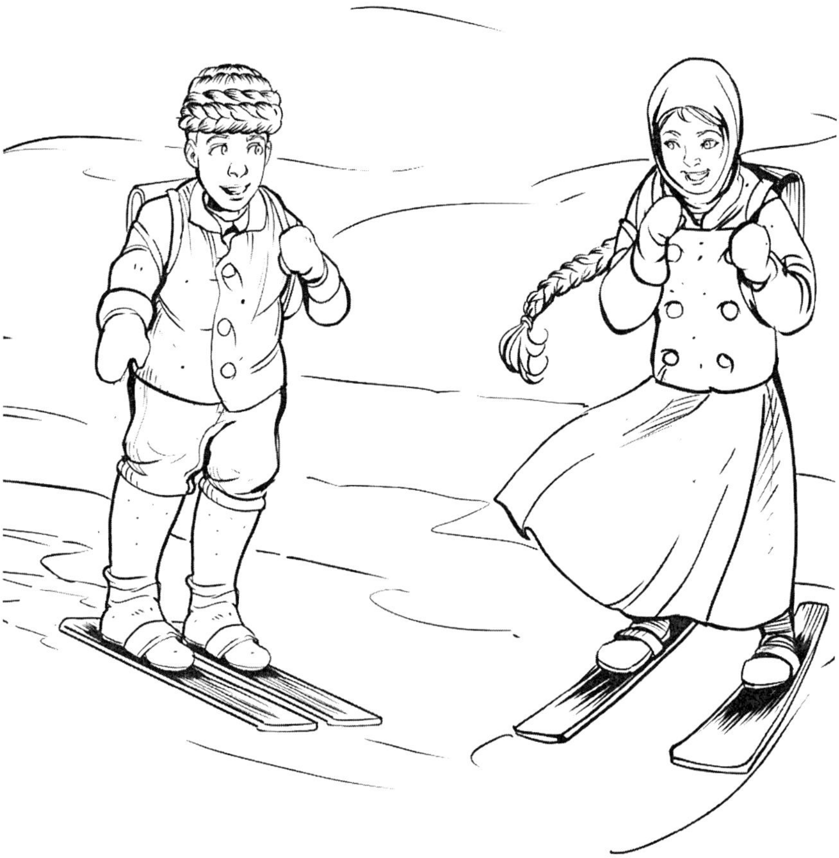

Chapter Four

That night, he told his mother he would be home late because he had to help Seija with a school project. He did not like lying to her, but it was for her gift.

"That is fine, but be home for dinner. I will have Hannu look after the animals for you. It is time he learned. You can show him tonight."

Hannu heard this and said, "I will do a better job than Markku does."

Markku frowned. "Do not worry about that, just do a good job. Put on your jacket, and we will go to the barn. I want to make sure you understand how to do the work."

Markku woke up the next morning excited about his mother's gift. He was not sure he knew what she needed. He would leave that to Mrs. Lilija.

He thought of his mother's gift at school all day. After saying goodbye to their friends, Markku skied home with Seija. Her mother was waiting at the door. "Hello, Mrs. Lilija."

"Hello, Markku. Please remove your boots and come in. I have pulla bread and warm milk for you."

"Thank you."

The pulla bread was homemade, like his mother's and tasted sweet. It had raisins in it too, with a little white frosting drizzled over the top. They sat at the table in the big room and enjoyed their snack.

"I have thought about the gift for your mother. I could knit her some warm socks. This winter has been so cold, and your mother takes the bus into town to shop. I think she will like some nice warm socks. You will need to work two Wednesdays for me. Grandma should be released from the hospital by then."

"Thank you, Mrs. Lilija."

That day, he cleaned the stalls, put down fresh straw, fed the animals, then carried in firewood and water. Mrs. Lilija waved good-bye as he skied away.

When he arrived home, everyone was sitting at the table, eating. His mother got up and dished up his food.

Mother frowned. "You are late. I thought you would be home for dinner."

"The project took longer than I thought. We will need to work on it again."

Another lie. He could not wait for Christmas, so he would not need to lie to his mother again.

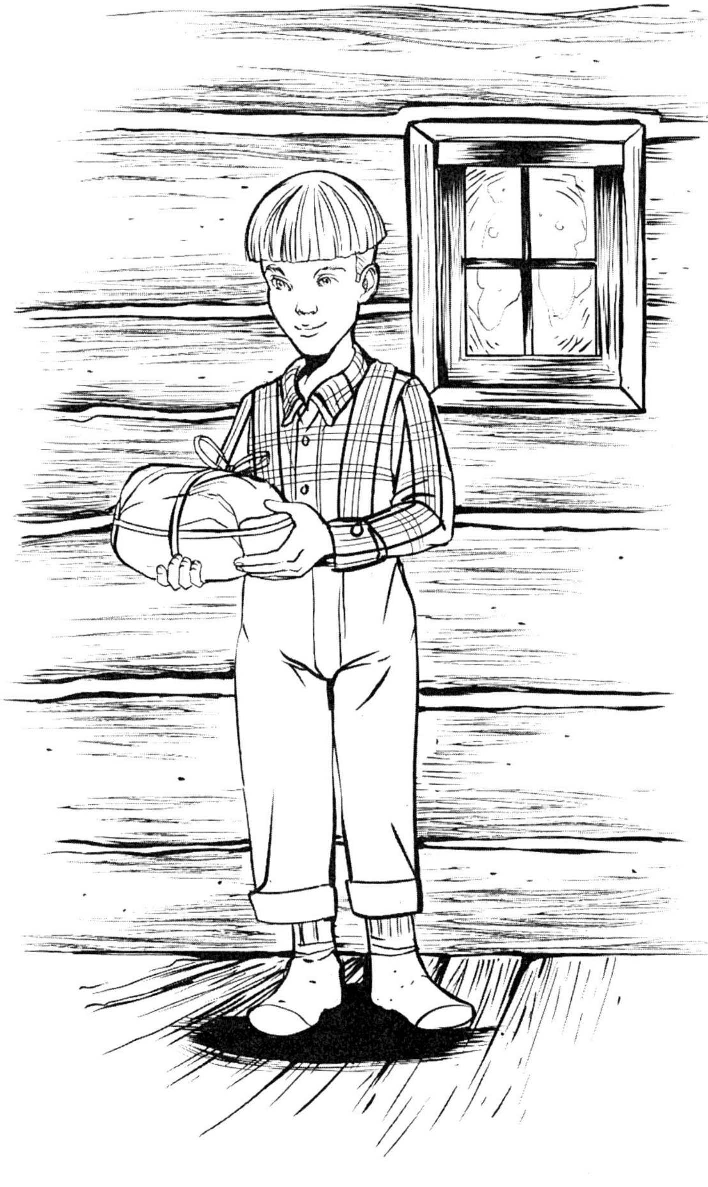

Chapter Five

On the next two Wednesdays, Markku left school and skied to the Lilija farm to start his work. He moved the animals out of their stalls and fed them. Then he raked out the old straw and put in new straw, while the animals ate. He needed two hours to do all his work and carry in the firewood and water. When the job was done, he shut the door, pulled down the latch and quickly skied home thinking of the nice warm socks he would give his mother.

He got home after his family had sat down to dinner. His mother always saved him a spot next to the stove. She dished up his dinner and patted him on the shoulder. He knew she was proud of him.

At school the following day, Seija told Markku her mother wanted to see him again. Markku skied home with her that afternoon. Thinking his mother would worry, he told his sister, Maikka, that he would be home late.

Mrs. Lilija had the socks for his mother on the kitchen table. They were beautiful Finnish blue with red and white squiggly lines running through them. The toes and heels were red.

"These are the most beautiful socks I have ever seen Mrs. Lilija!"

"Thank you, Markku. You did such a nice job for me. I made her a pair of mittens, too."

He smiled widely. He had a fine gift for his mother.

Mrs. Lilija wrapped the gifts in white paper and tied the package with a red ribbon. He put it in his book bag. When he got home, he hid the gift in the barn. He chose the top shelf and put it in the back. He could not wait for Christmas Eve!

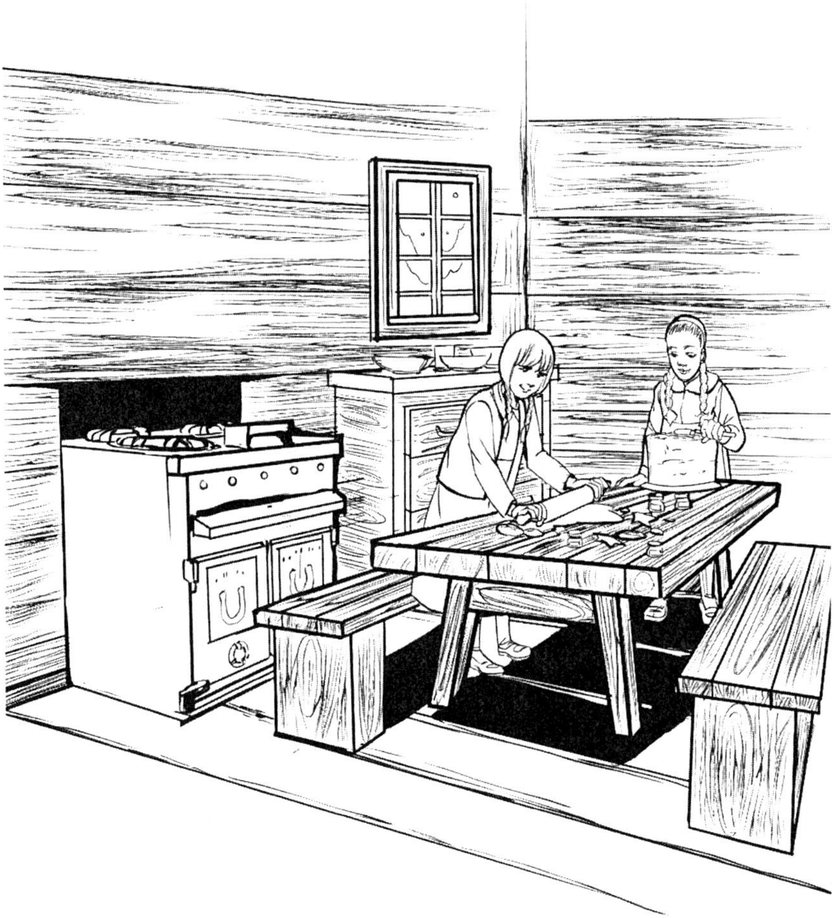

Chapter Six

Christmas was wonderful in their little farmhouse. Four weeks before Christmas, the baking started. Markku's mother and older sisters baked many different kinds of cookies and stored them in big bowls, then covered them with clean dish towels. Pulla coffee cakes were made with raisins or almonds and stored in cardboard boxes. The house smelled of ginger, vanilla, and sugar. The sweet smells made him hungry. His older sister, Maikka, sometimes sneaked him a cookie under the table. He ate it hungrily before his brothers and father came home for dinner.

Because he missed so much school, he sat at the kitchen table and studied most afternoons while they cut out cookies. Sometimes he grabbed a piece of cookie dough.

His mother had Hannu do his chores for an entire month. Hannu was proud of his work and told his mother, "I think I do a better job than Markku."

Mother hid her smile.

Markku knew how lucky he was to have a good home. Everyone worked hard for the family. He loved his brothers and sisters. His older sisters were not as crabby as Kauko's. He could do without his older brothers teasing him though. Every night one of them would knock him off the end of the bench when his mother was not looking. Older brothers could be so annoying. He knew the day would come when he would be as big and strong as they were. Then he could hold his spot on the bench. When he was older, he would not knock Hannu off the end of the bench. He knew that was not nice.

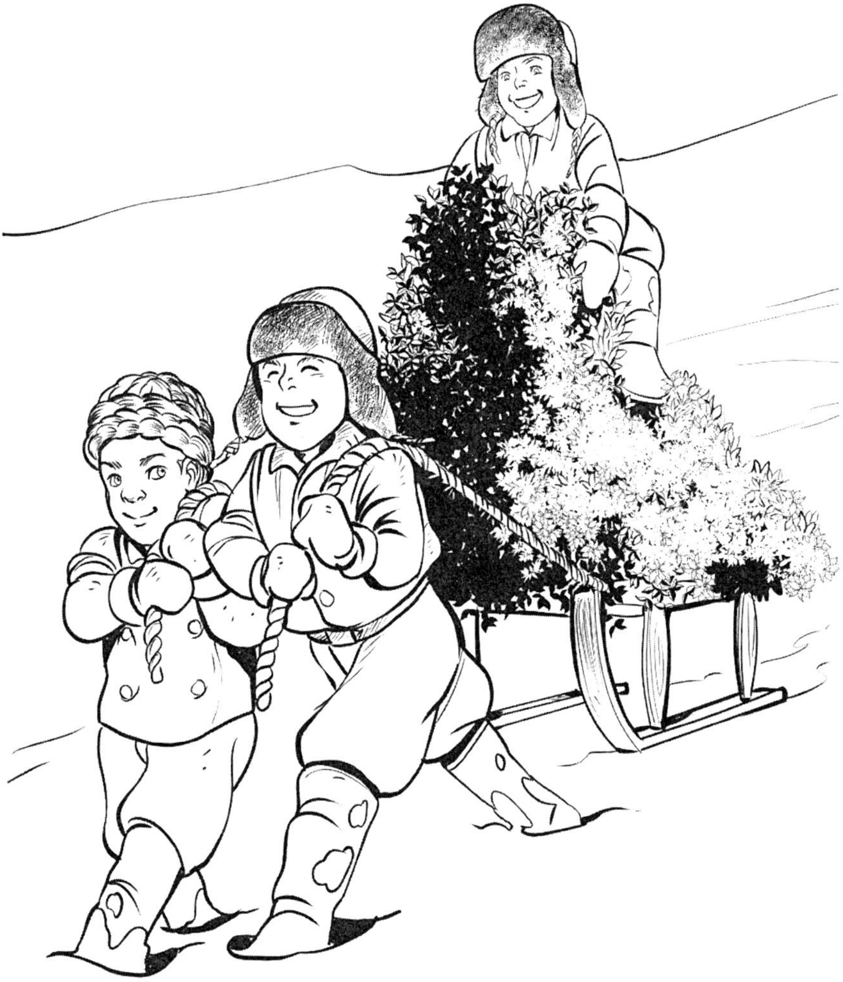

Chapter Seven

It was Christmas Eve day, and time to cut down the tree. Mother said Pauli, Markku, and Hannu could help if they did not go into the forest. There were lots of trees on the edge. His brothers had promised to look out for them.

Reijo and Ismo walked in front, tamping down the new snow for Pauli, Markku, and Hannu. They walked past the outhouse, barn, and sauna, to the edge of the woods. The branches bent down under the thick white blanket of snow. Reijo, being the oldest of the group, grabbed the trunk of the tree and shook it. Snow rained down on him. He would look at it and say, "What do you think of this one?"

The others would say "no," and they would move on to the next tree.

They had done this four times before they found the perfect Christmas tree. The trunk was straight, the branches were lush and green, and the height was perfect for their house.

The older brothers sawed the trunk back and forth until the tree fell over. They loaded it on the sled so the younger kids could tow it home. Hannu got to sit on the tree to hold it steady.

There were lots of smiles when the boys carried the tree into the house and set it up for their mother.

"Does this meet with your approval Mother? We cut down the best one for you."

"Yes, it is beautiful! Please set it in the corner. Tuula, Maikka, Tetta, you can bring over the decorations."

The decorations were apples, and cut out cookies, in shapes of hearts, little pigs, and stars. The girls had made chains from brown paper, and Mother brought out some white paper angels. She also clipped on some white candles, to be lit on Christmas Eve and Christmas Day.

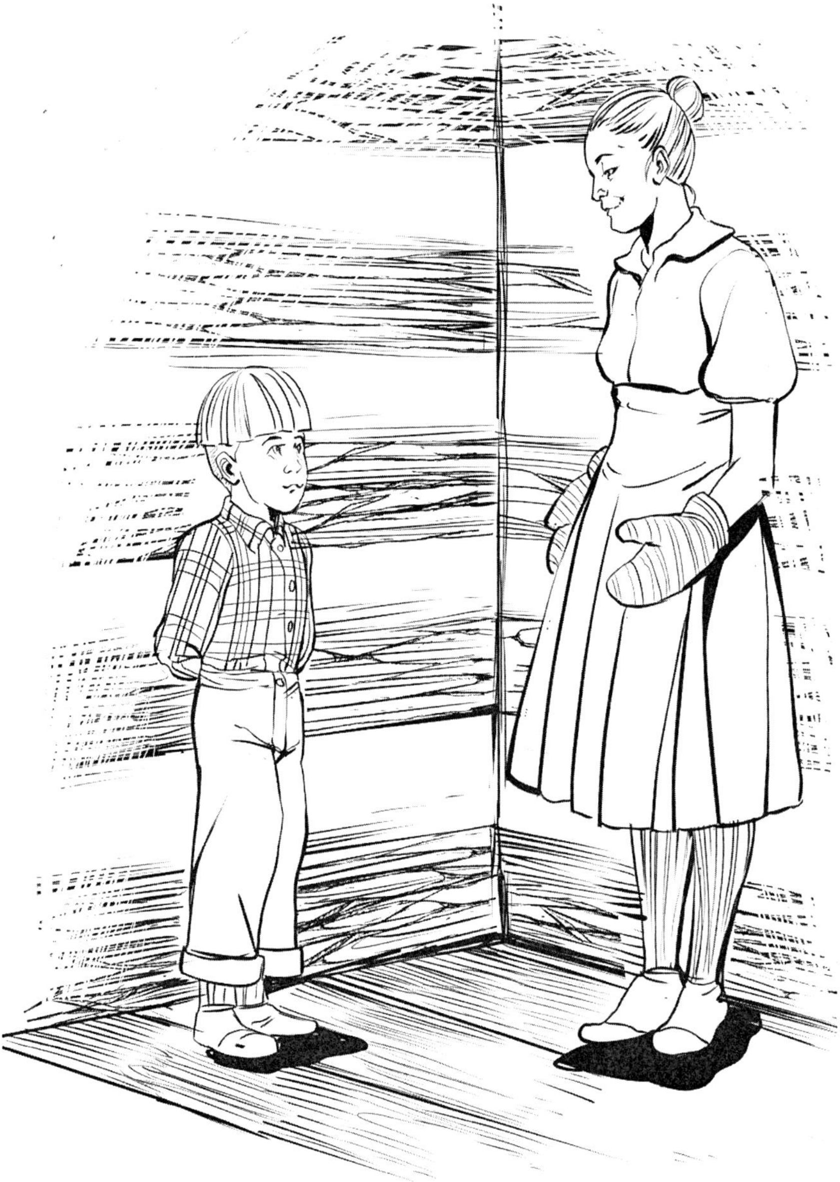

Chapter Eight

Christmas Eve dinner was special. They had lots of good food; smoked ham, mashed potatoes, carrots with butter, warm pulla slices, and plates of cookies and Christmas cakes.

After everyone had eaten, the older boys brought out a small gift box for their mother. She smiled and said, "Such a nice box. It is a pity to open it." She carefully untied the ribbon and lifted the lid to reveal several skeins of colorful yarn from the store in town. There was also a small bottle of cologne. Their mother was pleased.

"It is a nice gift from my boys, thank you."

Markku was not sure if his gift was good enough now. His brothers had given their mother such fine things. He frowned as his older brother Pentti said, "No reason to frown Markku. Bring out your gift for Mother."

How did he know he had a gift? He thought he had hidden it well in the barn. He got up and pulled his package out of his book bag.

"Here you are, something to make you smile."

Mother was surprised that Markku had a gift for her.

"What could be in this beautiful package? The red ribbon is so pretty."

She was surprised when she opened it and saw the hand knit socks and mittens. Immediately she tried them on and stood up. "Thank you, Markku for these warm gifts. My feet and hands will not freeze while I wait for the bus. Where did you get these?"

"I worked at Mrs. Lilija's farm a couple of afternoons, while she went into town to see her mother. She knitted them for me."

"Markku. You are growing into a young man." She gave him the biggest smile ever.

Then Father got a new pair of leather gloves from the boys and there were toys for the little kids. Hannu got a toy truck his father had carved from wood. The girls got little dolls made by their older sisters. The older girls got knitted mittens from Mother. After their gifts had been opened, Pentti lit the candles on the trees, and the girls sang.

Christmas Day, the neighbors stopped in, bringing their special Christmas foods. The long table was laden with meatballs, ham slices, mashed potatoes, cheeses, breads, beer, and lots of cookies and cakes. The kids drank homemade berry juice.

Markku saw his mother in the corner, showing her new socks and mittens to some of the ladies and thanking Mrs. Lillija for knitting them.

He heard Mrs. Lilija whisper to his mother, "He is a fine son, he wanted to make you smile."

After they had eaten, Pentti lit the candles on the tree, and they sang Christmas carols.

It was the best Christmas of Markku's life!

What are your favorite Christmas Memories?

_____
_____
_____
_____
_____
_____
_____
_____
_____
_____
_____

Markku

Markku, Pauli, and Maikka

Kaukko, Markku, and two friends

Majamaki Farm House

Where are they now?

All the children in this Finnish family worked hard on the farm. As is Finnish custom, the oldest son inherited the farm. The rest of the children found other work to do. The oldest sister, Tuula emigrated to California and one by one brought over each sibling who wanted to come. She started a daycare school, her sisters Maikka and Tetta worked for her.

The brothers Reijo, Ismo, and Pauli joined their sisters in California. They got jobs in construction and the automotive industry. Markku, who was the last one to move there, finished college, became an engineer, and designed machinery.

The youngest brother Hannu and the two baby girls, Sirpa and Pirrko, stayed in Finland. Hannu started a welding business. Sirpa and Pirkko became teachers.

Because they worked hard on the farm, they were successful in their careers. They continue to work hard and take care of their families.